Winner of:

The Distinguished Mom's Choice Award

New England Book Festival Honor

Los Angeles Book Festival Honor

San Francisco Book Festival Honor

Paris Book Festival Honor

Imagine · Dream · Believe

To: _Keira Ann Christ___

With Love:_____

Other books available by the author of *Twinkle Toes* for learning, sharing, and making special memories.

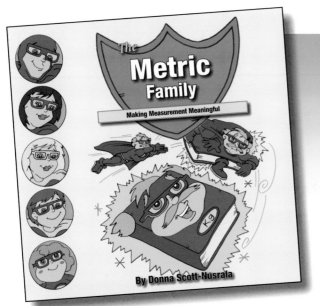

• 2011 Runner up Paris Book Festival

The Metric Family
Written by **Donna Scott-Nusrala**

Join Kilo, Hecto, Deka, Deci, Centi and Milli as they morph into Meters, Liters and Grams. Quickly make connections and clearly visualize each unit. *The Metric Family* teaches metrics with super heroes and rhyme. Learn name, order, size and abbreviation. Once you learn the family member's value and place, you can easily exchange units. Take the quiz at the end to see how well you understand the book. This is an excellent tool for self-teaching, classroom or home schooling.

Age 8 and up   32 pages   Paperback   Also available as an e-book

The Metric Family Learning Kit also available.
Includes the Metric Family book, step-by-step activities for meter, liter and gram, ml dropper, cups for estimating ml, cl, dcl, and dekaliter bucket. (Banner and bookmarks not shown.)

Gazillions, Bunches, Oodles and Tons
Written by **Donna Scott-Nusrala**   *Illustrated by* Kim Sponaugle

What will get rid of that pesky monster under the bed? *Gazillions, Bunches Oodles and Tons* of love of course. But how much is that? Is it enough? This is not the typical "I Love You" story. As you turn the page, kids hunt for the monster as it hides, shrinks and then scrambles out of the book. Watch fear disappear as love conquers the monster under the bed. Feel the infinite magnitude of love and share many types of hugs and kisses... "A story that kids will want to read over again..."

Ages 2 to 6   32 pages   Hardcover   Also available as an e-book

Twinkle Toes

By Donna Scott-Nusrala

Illustrated by Amy Rottinger

Stories I Love

A·M·O
PUBLISHING

To Contact Author:
Donna Scott-Nusrala

AMO PUBLISHING LLC
www.amopublishing.com
P.O. Box 10
Gates Mills, Ohio 44040

Library of Congress Control Number: 2010910804
ISBN: 978-0-9840227-0-0

Printed in the United States of America by
Bookmasters, Inc.
30 Amberwood Parkway
Ashland, Ohio 44805
October 2011   Job #M8989

This book is dedicated to Twinkle Toes and to Dreams

With love, gratitude and honor to:
Mom and Dad for immortalizing Twinkle Toes.
Patrick, Aaron, Dillon, Adam and Sarah.

We were jumping on the beds like popcorn in a hot pan. It was Christmas Eve and we were too excited to sleep. I was creaming my little cousin, Adam in a wild pillow fight.

Just as Grandma walked into the room … my pillow *EXPLODED*!

We froze. Feathers floated around us like a shaken snow globe.

We exchanged a grin and a wink with Grandma, and giggles escaped as we swept up the mess.

Then as if from nowhere, I tripped on a package. The tag read: *To Sarah, From T.T.*

I quickly opened it. "Yeah, new PJ's!" I cheered.

Adam tore his package open. "Pajamas? Why pajamas?" he said, resisting a yawn as he slipped them on.

I felt suddenly sleepy as I stretched my arm through the sleeve of my cozy, new pajamas.

"Wait a minute…Grandma…Who is T.T.?" I asked.

That was when she told us the best Christmas Eve story ever!

If you were to travel down the road just south of the North Pole and east a bit to the Land of Dreams, you might stumble upon a tiny farmhouse where smoke billows into the sky with a hint of peppermint.

Patches, a pocket sized calico keeps a keen eye on a pair of teeny twisted slippers. They belong to a fairy farmer named, Twinkle Toes.

Every year Twinkle Toes tills the snow. Then she piles rows and mounds just like any farmer would do in the dirt.

You won't find corn or pumpkins on the farm. Instead of seeds, Twinkle Toes plants fluffy fibers. She may add the hair of a puppy, the feather of a duck or even the tooth of a dinosaur, but she always adds a pinch of peppermint.

When all the planting is done, Twinkle Toes and Patches slip into the barn. Inside, she pulls a lever and with a *Flip…Flip…Flip* the windmill turns.

A loud *THUMP*…shakes the barn, followed by the sound of mixed radio waves…*RRRRRrrrrr…Blip…Blip…Blip…Blip.* She boots up the storm tracker and turns on the Dream Weaver.

Day after day, they record, watch and wait for just the right conditions. When…

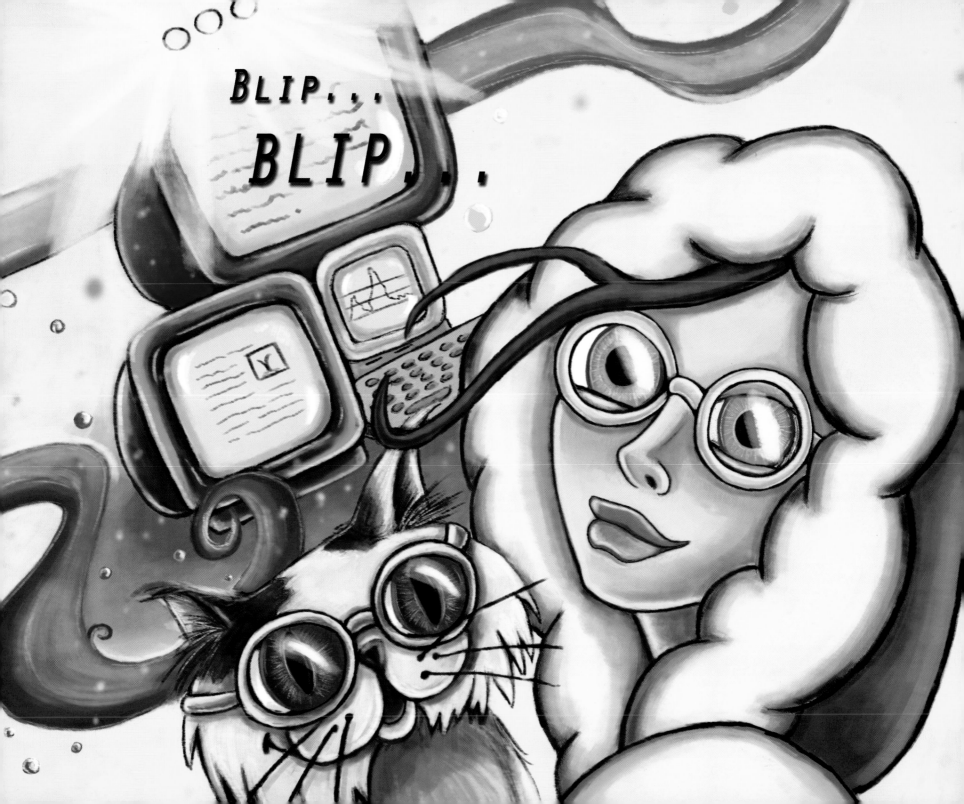

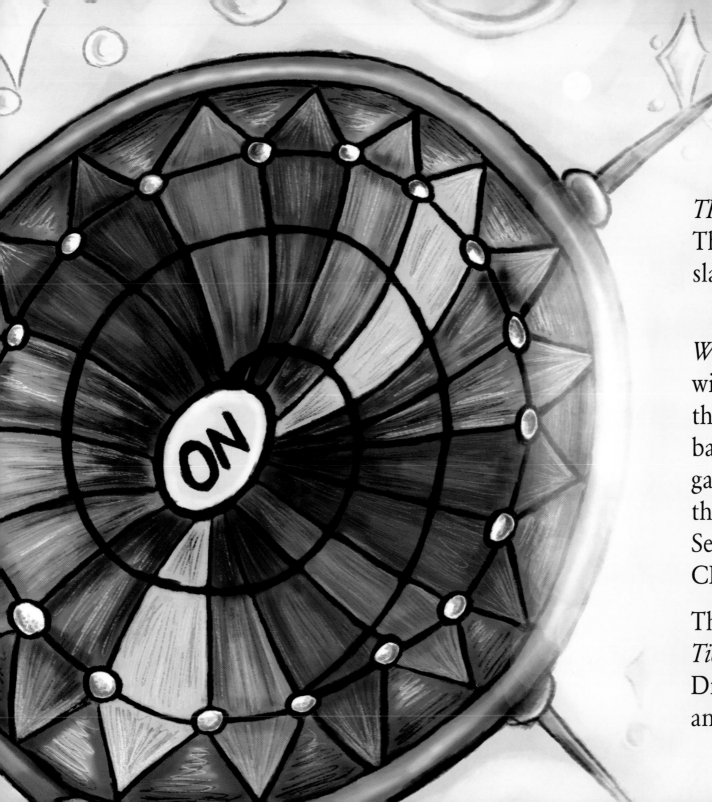

BOOM! THUD! THUD! BANG! The doors vibrate and slam.

Whoooooosh! WHOOOoooo! The wind hisses through the cracks in the barn. The storm gauge reads, mild… then moderate… Severe! Walloped! CLOBBERED!

Then, *Click…Click… Tick …Tick …* the Dream Weaver jerks and spins.

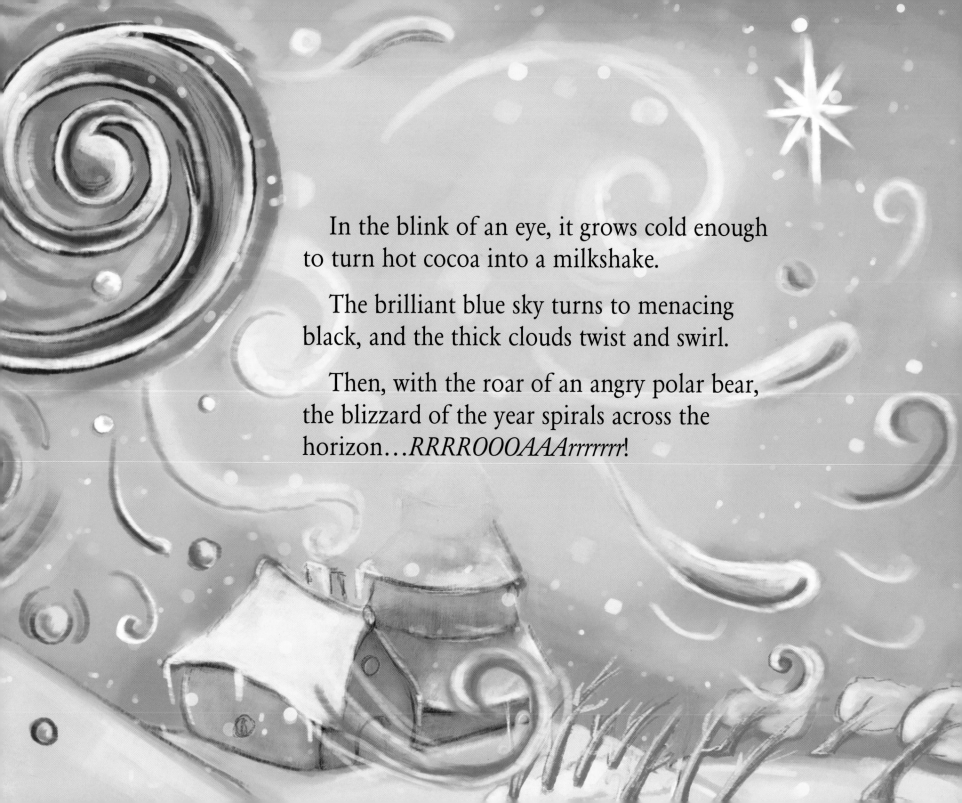

In the blink of an eye, it grows cold enough to turn hot cocoa into a milkshake.

The brilliant blue sky turns to menacing black, and the thick clouds twist and swirl.

Then, with the roar of an angry polar bear, the blizzard of the year spirals across the horizon…*RRRROOOAAArrrrrrr*!

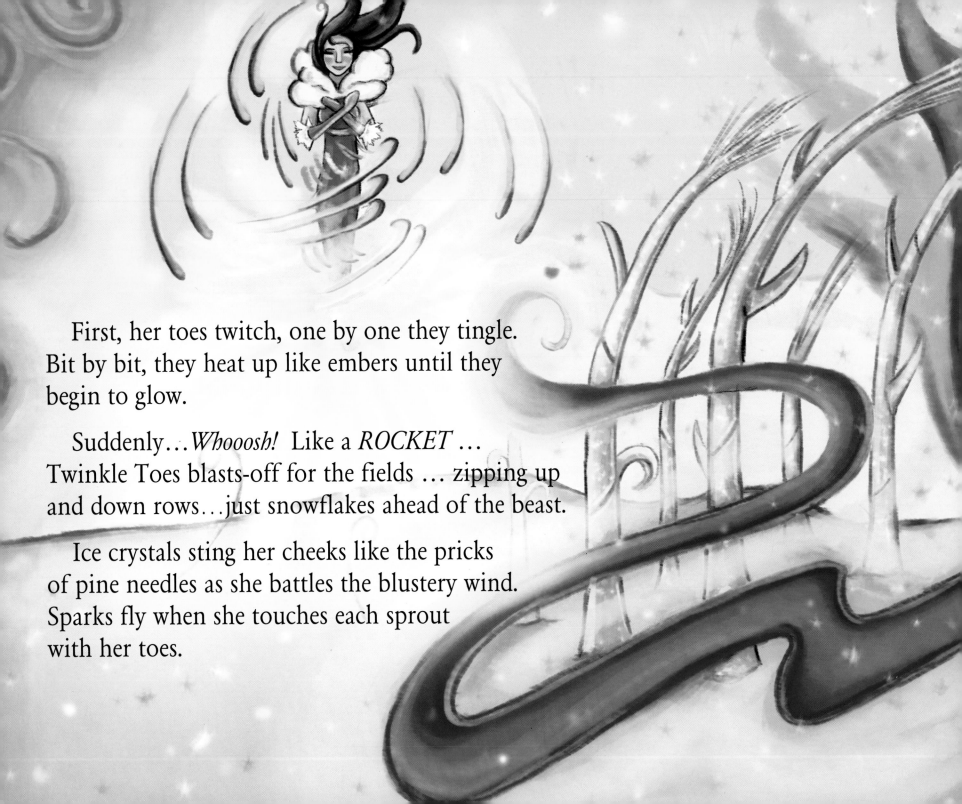

First, her toes twitch, one by one they tingle.
Bit by bit, they heat up like embers until they
begin to glow.

Suddenly…*Whooosh!* Like a *ROCKET* …
Twinkle Toes blasts-off for the fields … zipping up
and down rows…just snowflakes ahead of the beast.

Ice crystals sting her cheeks like the pricks
of pine needles as she battles the blustery wind.
Sparks fly when she touches each sprout
with her toes.

With a final burst and a flicker, she zooms inside, beating the blizzard by an eyelash. She crawls to her room and dives into bed. Patches purrs by her side.

They sleep for eleven days and eleven nights as the storm wails to a peak and then slows to a whimper.

As the last flake falls, a fountain of colored light spills through the clouds.

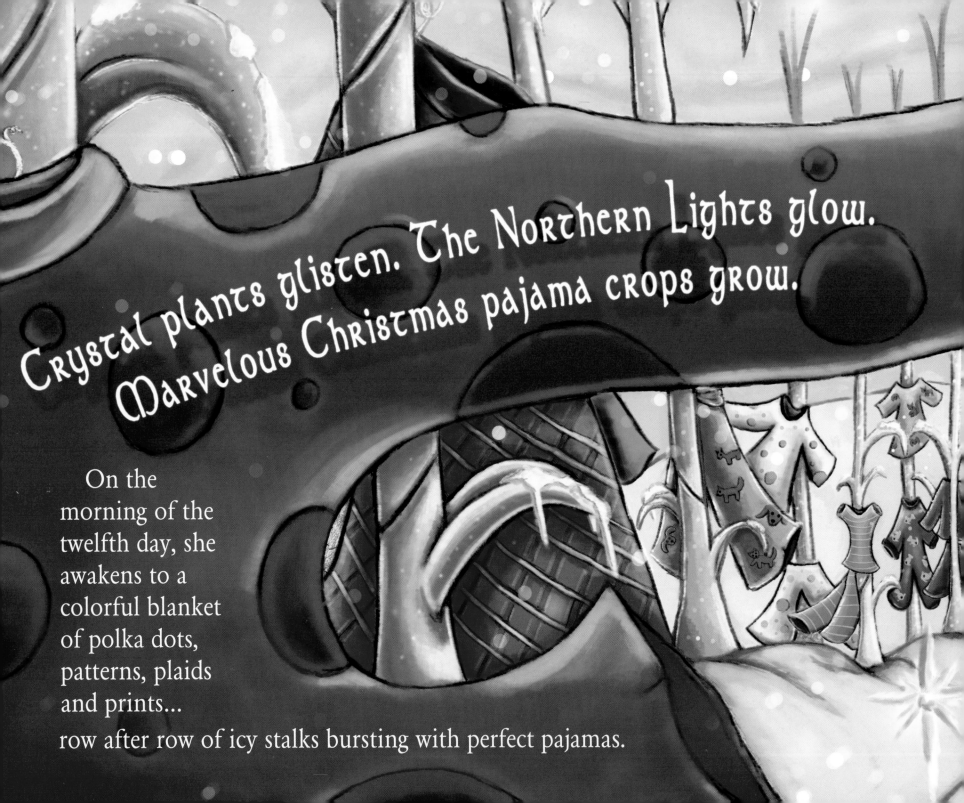

Crystal plants glisten. The Northern Lights glow.
Marvelous Christmas pajama crops grow.

On the morning of the twelfth day, she awakens to a colorful blanket of polka dots, patterns, plaids and prints...
row after row of icy stalks bursting with perfect pajamas.

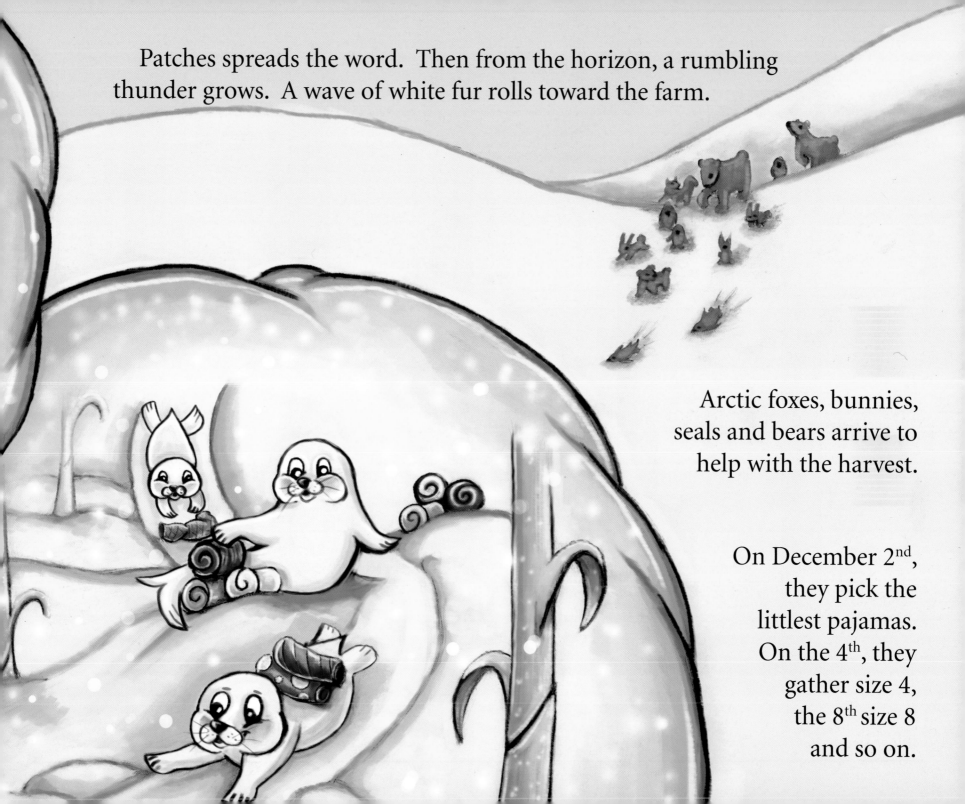

Patches spreads the word. Then from the horizon, a rumbling thunder grows. A wave of white fur rolls toward the farm.

Arctic foxes, bunnies, seals and bears arrive to help with the harvest.

On December 2nd, they pick the littlest pajamas. On the 4th, they gather size 4, the 8th size 8 and so on.

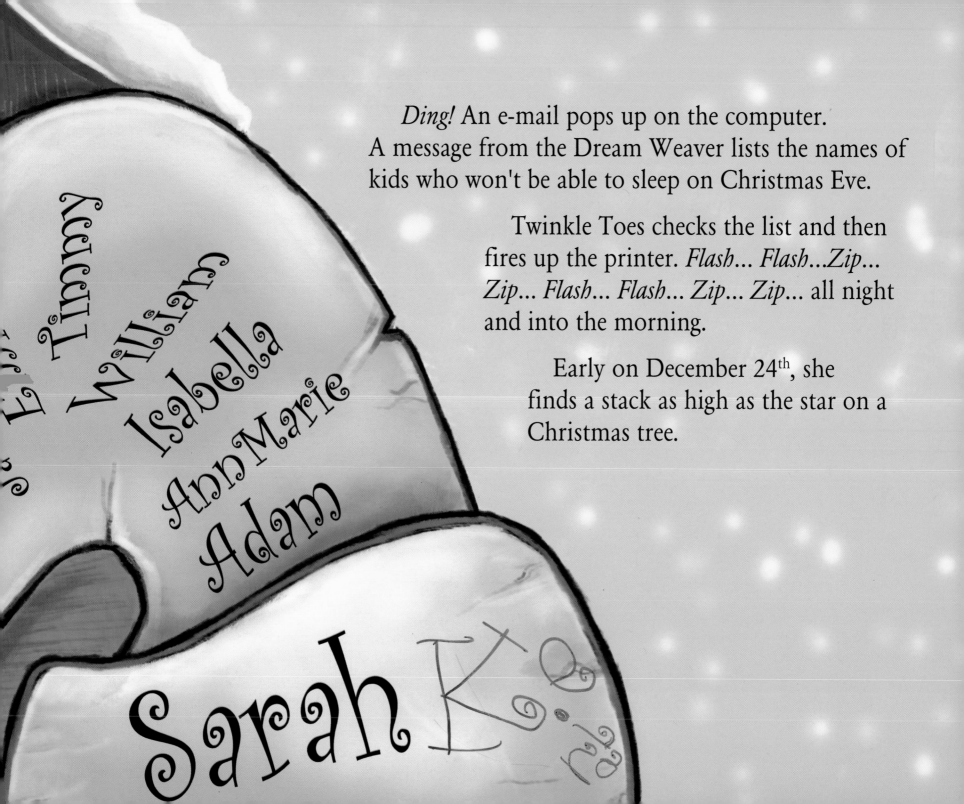

Ding! An e-mail pops up on the computer. A message from the Dream Weaver lists the names of kids who won't be able to sleep on Christmas Eve.

Twinkle Toes checks the list and then fires up the printer. *Flash... Flash...Zip... Zip... Flash... Flash... Zip... Zip...* all night and into the morning.

Early on December 24th, she finds a stack as high as the star on a Christmas tree.

Timmy

William

Isabella

AnnMarie

Adam

Sarah K.

She smiles at Patches, scratches his furry chin and says, "It's time to go!"

Patches fetches her downy, white parka. Twinkle Toes slips it on and then slides her arm through the handle of a crystal basket packed with pajamas.

Suddenly, her toes twitch. One by one, they tingle. Bit by bit, they heat up like embers until they start to glow.

Taking hold of the list, she soars through the sky like a rocket... *Whooooosh!*

She flits through a crack in the window and deposits a bundle on the bedroom floor. Then she disappears in a wink and a flash, leaving a hint of peppermint.

When fidgety, restless jumping beans get ready for bed, they discover a package addressed to them from, *T.T.*

They open cozy, warm pajamas that wear like a gentle hug. The soothing smell of peppermint settles the giggles and the wiggles.

Then with a stretch and a yawn, jumping beans become sleepy heads and the ants in their pants sneak away.

I was drifting off when…

"Sweet Dreams," Grandma said softly, closing the door.

I was awakened by Adam's voice in the dark. "Hey, Sarah," he whispered.

"What is it?" I replied.

"I smell peppermint," he said. "Do you smell peppermint, Sarah?"

I sniffed for a moment and thought, *That's funny… I do smell peppermint.*

When hopes become wishes, a dream grows.

A light of truth and promise glows.

T.T. is a member of the
American Dream Grower's Association